THE NIGHT BEFORE CHRISTMAS

WRITTEN BY
CLEMENT C. MOORE

RETOLD AND ILLUSTRATED BY
RACHEL ISADORA

G. P. PUTNAM'S SONS • PENGUIN YOUNG READERS GROUP

For David, Laura and Evan Lasker

'TWAS THE
NIGHT BEFORE
CHRISTMAS,

When all through the house
Not a creature was stirring,
not even a mouse.
The stockings were hung
by the chimney with care,
In hopes that St. Nicholas
soon would be there.

The children were nestled
all snug in their beds,
While visions of sugarplums
danced in their heads.

And mamma in her 'kerchief,
and I in my cap,
Had just settled our brains
for a long winter's nap,

When out on the lawn there arose such a clatter,
I sprang from the bed to see what was the matter.
Away to the window I flew like a flash,
Tore open the shutters and threw up the sash.

The moon on the breast of the new-fallen snow
Gave the luster of midday to objects below.
When, what to my wondering eyes should appear,
But a miniature sleigh and eight tiny reindeer,
With a little old driver so lively and quick,
I knew in a moment it must be St. Nick.

More rapid than eagles
his coursers they came,

And he whistled and shouted and called them by name!

"NOW, DASHER!

NOW, DANCER!

NOW, PRANCER

AND VIXEN!

ON, COMET! ON, CUPID!

ON, DONDER AND BLITZEN!

To the top of the porch!
To the top of the wall!
Now dash away! Dash away!
Dash away all!"
As dry leaves that before
the wild hurricane fly,
When they meet with
an obstacle, mount
to the sky,

So up to the housetop
the coursers they flew,
With the sleigh full of toys
and St. Nicholas too.

And then, in a twinkling,
I heard on the roof
The prancing and pawing
of each little hoof.

As I drew in my head and was
turning around,
Down the chimney St. Nicholas
came with a bound.

He was dressed all in fur from
his head to his foot,
And his clothes were all tarnished
with ashes and soot.

A bundle of toys he had
flung on his back,
And he looked like a peddler
just opening his pack.

His eyes, how they twinkled! His dimples, how merry!
His cheeks were like roses, his nose like a cherry!
His droll little mouth was drawn up like a bow,
And the beard of his chin was as white as the snow.
The stump of a pipe he held tight in his teeth,
And the smoke, it encircled his head like a wreath.

He had a broad face and a little round belly
That shook when he laughed, like a bowlful of jelly!
He was chubby and plump, a right jolly old elf,
And I laughed when I saw him, in spite of myself!

A wink of his eye and
a twist of his head
Soon gave me to know
I had nothing to dread.

He spoke not a word, but
went straight to his work,
And filled all the stockings,
then turned with a jerk,

And laying a finger aside of his nose,
And giving a nod, up the chimney he rose!

He sprang to his sleigh, to his team gave a whistle,
And away they all flew like the down of a thistle.
But I heard him exclaim, ere he drove out of sight,

"HAPPY CHRISTMAS TO ALL,

AND TO ALL
A GOOD-NIGHT!"

G. P. PUTNAM'S SONS
A division of Penguin Young Readers Group. Published by The Penguin Group. Penguin Group (USA) Inc., 375 Hudson Street, New York, NY 10014, U.S.A.
Penguin Group (Canada), 90 Eglinton Avenue East, Suite 700, Toronto, Ontario M4P 2Y3, Canada (a division of Pearson Penguin Canada Inc.).
Penguin Books Ltd, 80 Strand, London WC2R 0RL, England.
Penguin Ireland, 25 St. Stephen's Green, Dublin 2, Ireland (a division of Penguin Books Ltd.).
Penguin Group (Australia), 250 Camberwell Road, Camberwell, Victoria 3124, Australia (a division of Pearson Australia Group Pty Ltd).
Penguin Books India Pvt Ltd, 11 Community Centre, Panchsheel Park, New Delhi - 110 017, India.
Penguin Group (NZ), 67 Apollo Drive, Rosedale, North Shore 0632, New Zealand (a division of Pearson New Zealand Ltd).
Penguin Books (South Africa) (Pty) Ltd, 24 Sturdee Avenue, Rosebank, Johannesburg 2196, South Africa.
Penguin Books Ltd, Registered Offices: 80 Strand, London WC2R 0RL, England.

Published simultaneously in Canada. Manufactured in China by South China Printing Co. Ltd.
Design by Marikka Tamura. Text set in Geist.
The illustrations were done with oil paints, printed paper and palette paper.
Library of Congress Cataloging-in-Publication Data
Moore, Clement Clarke, 1779–1863.
The night before Christmas / by Clement C. Moore ; retold and illustrated by Rachel Isadora.
p. cm. 1. Santa Claus—Juvenile poetry. 2. Christmas—Juvenile poetry. 3. Children's poetry, American. I. Isadora, Rachel, ill. II. Title.
PS2429.M5N5 2009 811'.2—dc22 2008053359
ISBN 978-0-399-25408-6
1 3 5 7 9 10 8 6 4 2